NO WORRIES!

AN ACTIVITY BOOK FOR YOUNG PEOPLE WHO SOMETIMES FEEL ANXIOUS OR STRESSED

Kane Miller
A DIVISION OF EDC PUBLISHING

Kane Miller
A DIVISION OF EDC PUBLISHING

First American Edition 2018
Kane Miller, A Division of EDC Publishing

© 2017 Studio Press
Consultant Dr. Sharie Coombes, Child, Family & Adult Psychotherapist,
Ed.D, MA (PsychPsych), DHypPsych(UK), Senior QHP, B.Ed.
Written by Lily Murray
Illustrated by Katie Abey
Designed by Rob Ward

First published in the UK in 2017 by Studio Press,
an imprint of Bonnier Books UK

For information contact:
Kane Miller, A Division of EDC Publishing
PO Box 470663
Tulsa, OK 74147-0663
www.kanemiller.com
www.edcpub.com
www.usbornebooksandmore.com

Library of Congress Control Number: 2017942235

Printed in China
8 9 10

ISBN: 978-1-61067-710-3

THIS BOOK BELONGS TO

_ _ _ _ _ _ _ _ _

WELCOME TO NO WORRIES!

Consultant
DR. SHARIE COOMBES
Child and Family Psychotherapist

We all have worries from time to time, and this fun activity book is a great way to get you thinking and talking about the things that make you feel worried, so you can get on with being you and enjoying life. The pages show you how to push those worries away and will give you ideas about how to feel better.

Use this book in a quiet, relaxed place where you can think and feel comfortable. The activities will help you understand your feelings, feel calmer, talk to others about your worries (if you want to) and grow in courage and positivity. It's up to you which pages you do, and you can start anywhere in the book. You can do a page a day if that's what you want, or complete lots of pages at once. You can come back to a page many times. There are no rules!

Sometimes worries can feel really big, and we think nothing will help. That's exactly what the worries want us to think, but there is a solution to every problem. Nothing is so big that it can't be sorted out or talked about, even if it feels that way. Remember, you are definitely stronger than your worries, so if you find yourself worrying so much that it gets difficult to enjoy yourself, you could show some of these activities to important people in your life to help you explain how you are feeling and to get help with what is upsetting you. You can also always talk to an adult you trust at school or home, who can take you to the doctor to get some help.

Lots of children need a bit of extra help every now and then, and there are organizations you can turn to if you don't want to talk to people you know. They have helped thousands of people with every imaginable problem and will know how to support you without judging you.

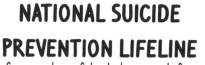

CRISIS TEXT LINE

Serves anyone, in any type of crisis, providing access to free, 24/7 support.
Connect with a trained crisis counselor to receive free, 24/7 crisis support via text message. Text HELLO to 741741

www.crisistextline.org

NATIONAL SUICIDE PREVENTION LIFELINE

24/7, free and confidential support for people in distress. Call free or chat online.
No matter what problems you're dealing with, whether or not you're thinking about suicide, if you need someone to lean on for emotional support or are worried about a friend or loved one call the Lifeline.
www.suicidepreventionlifeline.org
1-800-273-8255

Imagine that you're about to go out for the day.
What things might make you feel anxious?
Write or draw them on the picture above.

THE VENUS WORRY-TRAP

Once the seed of a worry is planted it can easily grow into a big anxiety.

Imagine that this Venus flytrap has grown from one of your worries.

The more you think about what's making you feel nervous, the quicker and bigger the worry-trap plant will grow.

Write the name of your worry on the pot, then add some worry words or sentences around the plant that might have made it grow bigger.

Look at all the words you've been feeding the worry plant.

Are any of them **100%** true?

Write down things you can think or do to change what you're feeding the plant. The worry plant doesn't like positive thoughts!

WEED KiLLER

100% EFFECTiVE!

Next time you feel anxious, try to replace your worry thoughts with positive ones.

ANXIETY ON THE OUTSIDE

Look at the worry word search. When anxiety is pushing its way in, do you get any of these feelings?

DIZZY

RACING HEART

COLD

SICK

TEARFUL

SWEATY

HEADACHE

TIGHT THROAT

FAINT

WEAK

F	A	C	S	H	B	W	O	Q	H	T	G
D	D	M	K	W	C	O	L	D	R	G	U
J	T	C	B	U	E	O	Z	A	Z	M	X
I	I	E	C	X	H	A	E	U	C	K	P
S	Q	E	A	Z	B	H	T	Y	D	T	E
Z	M	Z	E	R	G	B	I	Y	H	M	H
H	A	I	G	N	F	N	A	V	J	J	K
V	F	A	I	N	T	U	D	I	X	A	B
I	S	C	O	J	K	N	L	I	E	B	Q
O	A	Q	I	G	N	H	E	W	Z	O	U
R	H	E	A	D	A	C	H	E	D	Z	N
T	I	G	H	T	T	H	R	O	A	T	Y

When people think about being nervous or anxious, they often think about it as an emotion that's in their head, but anxiety can often be felt in your body.

On the picture below, write or draw on the parts of the body where you feel anxiety.

How do you think noticing your anxious feelings when they begin might help you?

WORRY FEELINGS

Being worried can produce different kinds of feelings. It can make you feel angry or shouty or sad, or want to go somewhere quiet on your own.

All these people are showing different emotions because they are worried. Write down what they might be thinking about.

I'm worried about
....
....
....

I wish I could stop thinking about
....
....

You're not my friend anymore.

I'm feeling sad because
....
....

Go away!

I'm sad about
....
....
....

It helps if you think about how people around you are feeling too.
Everyone has worries of their own that they might not tell you about, even grown-ups.

WORRY MONKEYS

The worry monkeys are frightened about something. Search and find each worry monkey, then cheer them up by coloring them in.

THE WORRY JAR

What do you worry about? Fill a jar with your worries, then screw the lid on tight to stop them from getting out!

Write or draw your worries on slips of paper, then put the slips in an empty jar.

You can do this on your own, or share a jar. Ask a friend or family member about their worries.

LAUGHTER IS GOOD FOR THE SOUL

DRAW OR WRITE SOMETHING
THAT MAKES YOU LAUGH.

DOODLE FACES

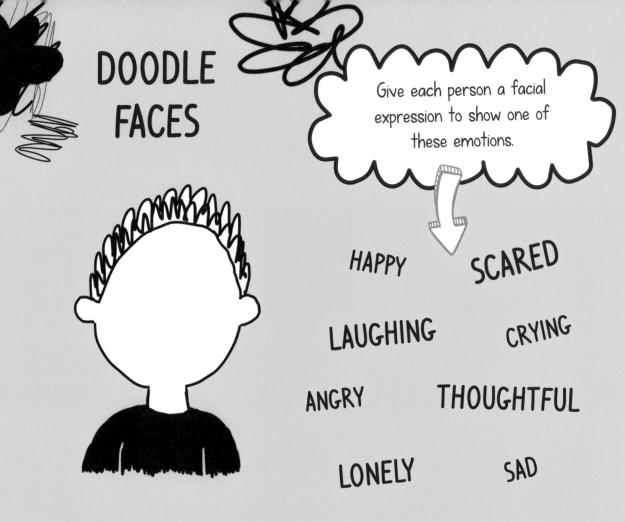

Give each person a facial expression to show one of these emotions.

HAPPY   SCARED

LAUGHING   CRYING

ANGRY   THOUGHTFUL

LONELY   SAD

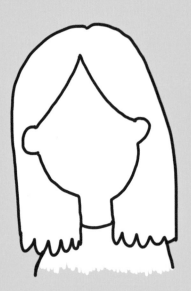

NATURE DAYDREAM

Close your eyes and imagine yourself outside in a beautiful place. Where are you? A meadow, a forest, on the beach?

Would you like someone with you, or would you rather be alone?
What sounds do you think you can hear?
Draw or write your nature daydream below.

MY WORRIED FACE

DRAW A PICTURE OF HOW YOU THINK YOU LOOK WHEN YOU'RE WORRIED.

WORRY LISTS

Some worries are about things that are definitely going to happen, like a test or a trip. But other worries can be things that are very unlikely to happen.

Think about your worries and see if you can put them into these two lists:

WORRIES THAT MIGHT HAPPEN

WORRIES THAT WILL PROBABLY NEVER HAPPEN

You can make a plan for fighting these worries.

Remind yourself that really bad things often don't happen.

WHAT DO YOU WANT TO SAY TO THE WORRIES THAT ARE PROBABLY NEVER GOING TO HAPPEN?

WORRY MONSTERS

Imagine your worries as little monsters.

What might one of your worry monsters look like?

Is it hairy with sharp claws, or is it more like a slimy blob that keeps sticking to you?

Does it have lots of eyes or a long nose?

Now think of lots of ways you can get rid of your worry monsters.

STEP ON THEM

SQUASH THEM

Blow them away

LOCK Them in a cage

Trap them

PUT THEM IN A JAR

THINK POSITIVE

The best thing to do about worries
is to talk about them ...
and then ignore them!

Draw pictures of all the things you
could be doing instead of thinking
about your worries.

COLOR THESE IN

Use any
colors you like.

Try different colors
for each pattern or color
them all the same.

WHAT CAN YOU HEAR?

When you're at home and there's lots going on around you, try closing your eyes and listening for a minute.

What can you hear? Music? Talking? What are people saying?

Draw or write all the things you can hear.

Think of one of your happiest memories. It could be a family celebration, a day with friends, a trip, the time your team won a game, or any moment when you're happiest, such as reading or playing sports.

GREAT MEMORIES!

Write or draw your happy memory in the box below.

Find someone to show your memory to and tell them all about it.

Next time you're feeling worried, try thinking about this memory instead and picture it in your mind.

WRITE A LETTER TO SOMEONE YOU LOVE, TELLING THEM WHY THEY ARE GREAT.

Here are some words to help you get started:

THOUGHTFUL

chatty

caring

interesting

helpful

KIND

give good hugs

FORGIVING

make me laugh

INTERESTED

funny

good at listening

loving

FUN

inspiring

FRIENDSHIPS

Write down the names of your favorite people or pets.

Write what you like best about them.

Next time you see them, tell them.

Ask your friends what they like best about you and write down the things they say.

WHAT ABOUT ME?

COLOR THIS IN

I AM
LOVED

TAKE A BREATH!

Try this breathing exercise to help you relax:

STEP 1

Make sure you are sitting comfortably in a quiet and safe place. When you feel ready, close your eyes. Notice your breathing. Think about how it feels breathing in and breathing out. Try to breathe in through your nose and out through your mouth.

STEP 2

Place your hand on your stomach and focus on the feeling of it rising and falling with each breath. When you breathe in, quietly say "in" to yourself, and when you breathe out, quietly say "and out" to yourself.

STEP 3

Concentrate on nothing but your breathing and try to let go of any other thoughts you may have.

After you've practiced the breathing exercise a lot, next see if you can think about a happy memory while you're doing it. Then your happy memory will take up all the space in your brain, and there won't be any room for worries.

DO THIS FOR 2 MINUTES

WHAT CAN YOU HEAR OUTSIDE?

Go outside, whatever the weather. If it's rainy, find a sheltered spot; if it's cold, put on your warmest clothes.

Sit in silence for a while and close your eyes, listening to the sounds around you.

Write down the noises you hear.

COMPLETE THE PICTURE

Imagine a calm lake. Are there boats on the water? Is the sun setting? Is the sky filled with stars?

RELAX   Try this relaxation exercise:

1. Lie down on the floor and close your eyes.

2. Begin by breathing in through your nose. Hold your breath for a few seconds, then breathe out. Take another deep breath through your nose. Imagine your stomach is a balloon filling with air and then as you breathe out, imagine all the air escaping.

3. Stretch out your legs in front of you, pointing your toes. Stretch out your arms on either side of you, stretching all the way through to your fingertips.

4. Now start to tense all the muscles in your body. Begin with your toes. Curl them over so they're clenched. Then think about tensing the muscles all the way up your legs and through your stomach. Imagine something is about to step on your stomach and you want to make it into a hard wall.

5. Tense your arms so they are by your sides and even your fists are clenched. Bring your shoulders up around your ears.

6. Last of all, scrunch up your face. Push your lips together and frown really hard so your forehead is crinkled.

7. Now, make your body go limp again. Let your legs and arms go loose. Relax your shoulders by bringing them down. Imagine yourself as a floppy rag doll.

8. Take a deep breath in through your nose and breathe out again. Notice how relaxed and calm you feel and then, when you're ready, open your eyes.

DOODLES

Fill every single space on this page with doodles. Let your mind wander!

IMAGINE THAT YOUR FEELINGS ARE LIKE THE WEATHER

Feeling sad could be a rainy day, anger could be a thunderstorm and happiness could be sunshine. Write a weather report or draw a picture of how you felt at different times today.

COLOR YOUR FEELINGS

Do you think feelings have their own colors? Color in each of these feeling words with the color that you think suits them best.

ANGER

Happy

Sad

FEAR

Laughter

WORRY

EMPTY YOUR MIND

Empty your mind completely by focusing on this spot.

When your mind is empty, think about your five senses – touch, taste, sight, hearing and smell.

Fill in the sentences below for each sense:

I smell...

I hear...

I feel...

I see...

I taste...

COLOR THESE IN

THE HAPPY JAR

Fill this jar with happiness by writing or drawing happy thoughts and pictures.

You can fill the jar with words, sentences, drawings, or a mixture of all three.

ALL ABOUT ME!

Write a list of the things you like about yourself.

Choose anything—your best qualities, your personality, or things you are good at.

COLOR THIS WORD AND DOODLE AROUND IT,
DRAWING THINGS THAT MAKE YOU HAPPY

HAPPINESS

FLY AWAY YOUR WORRIES

Write down your worries on these paper airplanes.

After you've written your worries, cut along the dotted line at the side of the page, then fold your paper airplane along the numbered lines.

When you are finished, ask an adult to help you cut them and then send them on their way, out of your life.

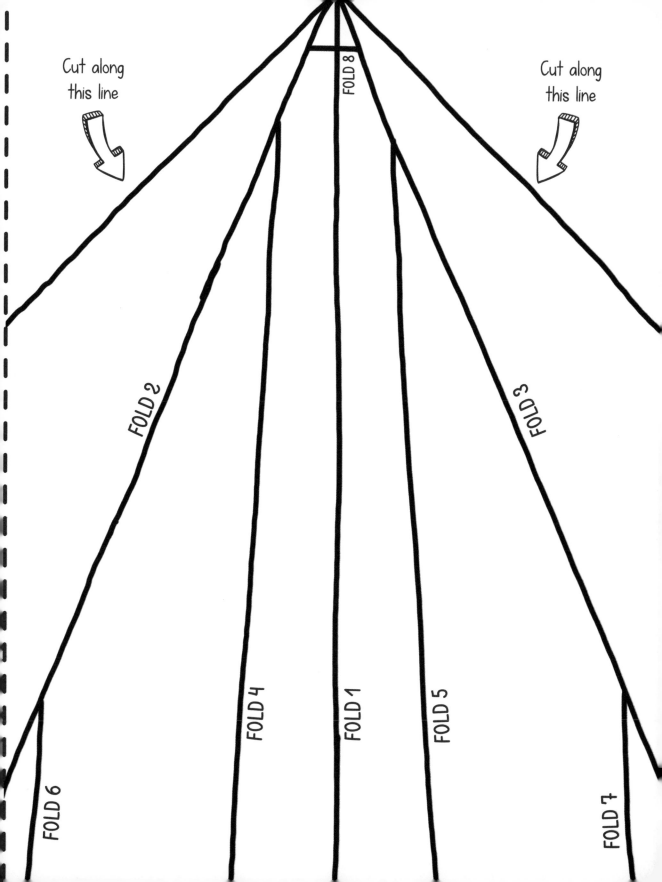

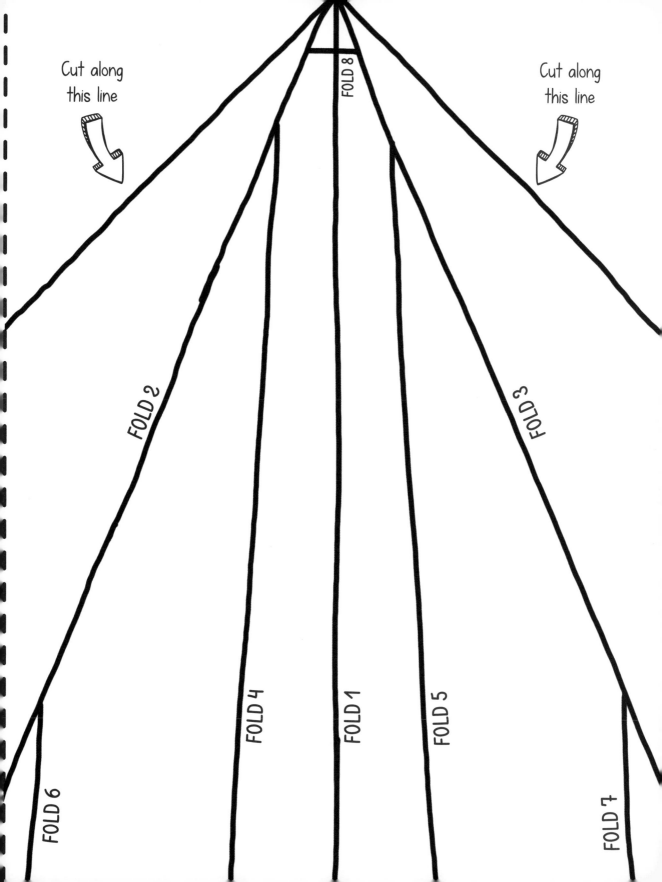

Cut along
this line

Cut along
this line

FOLD 8

FOLD 2

FOLD 3

FOLD 4

FOLD 1

FOLD 5

FOLD 6

FOLD 7

HA!

CHUCKLE BOX

Fill this box with things that make you laugh.

FEELING ACTIVE

Exercise can help make you feel better. Try doing one of these exercises every day:

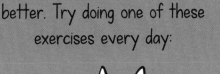

20 JUMPING JACKS

Stand tall with your feet together and your hands at your sides. Quickly raise your arms above your head while jumping your feet out to the sides. Then immediately bring your arms back down to your sides and jump so your feet are together again.

30 ARM CIRCLES

Stand up straight with your arms stretched out on either side of your body. Slowly move your arms in circles without rotating your wrists or elbows.

8 SQUATS

Stand with your feet hip-width apart, hands on your hips, and slowly sink down, bending at your knees and hips. Make sure your back is straight, and sink as low as possible without letting your knees go past the ends of your toes. Then slowly rise back to standing position.

10 CALF RAISES

With your feet spaced hip-width apart, place your hands on your hips and lift your heels off the ground. Standing on tip-toe count to eight, slowly lower back down, then return your feet to the floor.

10 LUNGES

Take a step forward and bend so that your back knee touches the floor. Make sure your front knee doesn't bend past your toes.

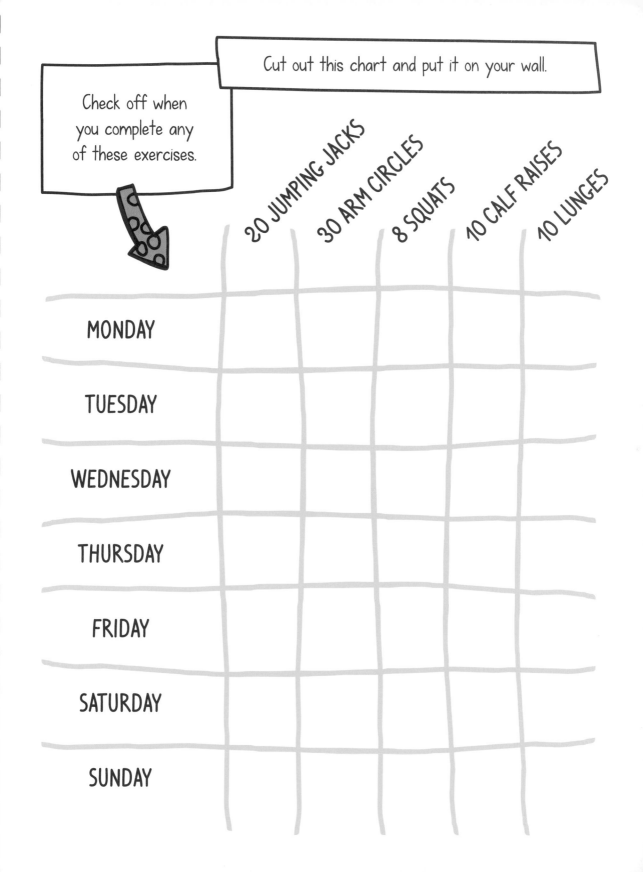

Check off when you complete any of these exercises.

Cut out this chart and put it on your wall.

20 JUMPING JACKS

30 ARM CIRCLES

8 SQUATS

10 CALF RAISES

10 LUNGES

MONDAY

TUESDAY

WEDNESDAY

THURSDAY

FRIDAY

SATURDAY

SUNDAY

WORRY FREE

Draw yourself without worries. How does it feel? Better? Who will be the first to notice you've let your worries go?

COLOR THESE IN

DESERT ISLAND DOODLES

Draw what you would take to a desert island.

What things are most important to you?

Who would you take if you could choose three people?

WHEN I AM OLDER

Write down all the things you want
to do when you're older.

DRAW A PICTURE ON THIS PAGE USING A PENCIL OR A BALLPOINT PEN.

Don't lift the pencil from the page and press as hard as you can without tearing the paper.

Now turn the page to see the embossed effect your drawing has made.

THIS IS YOUR EMBOSSED ARTWORK.
GIVE IT A NAME.

I CALL THIS ARTWORK...

RIP OUT THIS PAGE AND TEAR IT INTO AS MANY TEENY TINY PIECES AS YOU CAN, THEN THROW THEM INTO THE RECYCLING!

Write a thank-you letter to someone,
saying thank you for something they have done for you.

HUGS!

Hugs are good for the soul.
Who would you like to hug right now?

Close your eyes and imagine it.

How does it make you feel?

Are you happy?
Comforted? Content?

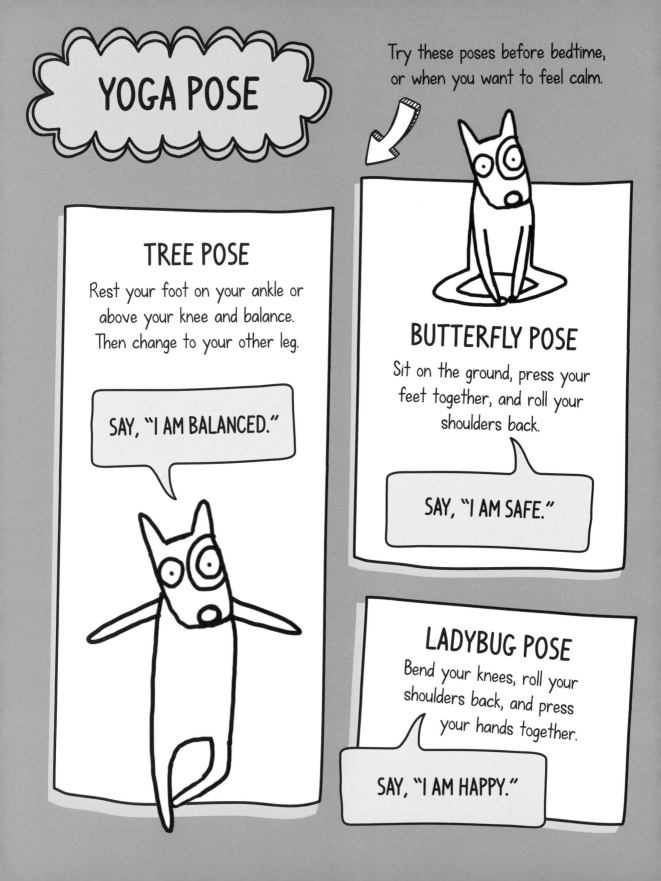

YOGA POSE

Try these poses before bedtime, or when you want to feel calm.

TREE POSE

Rest your foot on your ankle or above your knee and balance. Then change to your other leg.

SAY, "I AM BALANCED."

BUTTERFLY POSE

Sit on the ground, press your feet together, and roll your shoulders back.

SAY, "I AM SAFE."

LADYBUG POSE

Bend your knees, roll your shoulders back, and press your hands together.

SAY, "I AM HAPPY."

CHILD'S POSE

Bend your legs, fold your body onto your thighs and either rest your arms by your sides or extend them in front of you, whichever feels more comfortable.

SAY, "I AM AT REST."

CAT POSE

Breathe in and look up, letting your back drop down. Breathe out and tuck in your chin, lifting your back in a high arch.

SAY, "I AM AT EASE."

SLEEP POSE

Lie on your back and take slow breaths. Close your eyes if you want. Try to empty yourself of thoughts. If your mind wanders away, notice where it goes, then bring your attention back to your breathing.

SAY, "I AM AT HOME."

CALM COLORING

Imagine, draw and color a peaceful
underwater world filled with cool water,
swimming fish, bubbling coral,
small shells and swaying seaweed.

LISTEN TO THE BELL

Ring a bell, or fill a glass half-full with water and run your finger along the rim of the glass until it makes a ringing sound. Listen carefully until you can no longer hear it.

TAKE A WALK

What can you see?

For one minute of the walk, stay completely still and look at all the things around you.

Write down or draw what you saw. It could be anything – a red car, a lawn mower, a bird.

THANK-YOU MOMENTS

Find a moment every day to say "thank you" for all the good things in your life.

family

friends

pets

home

toys

food

clubs

bedroom

school

teachers

soccer

running

Write down all the things you feel grateful to have in your life.

You could try saying thank you at mealtimes, when everyone is gathered together.

Or you could ask friends or family to share one thing they're thankful for each day.

Or you could say all the things you're thankful for at bedtime.

RHYME TIME!

Think of as many rhyming word pairs as you can and write them below.

Then write a poem on the next page using the word pairs to show how you are feeling today.

WHALE   TAIL

Create your
poem here.

COLOR THIS IN

YOUR SAFE PLACE

Draw or attach a picture of somewhere you feel completely safe and happy.

Your safe place could be somewhere you've seen or been to, heard about, read about or dreamed about. A special, safe place where everything feels peaceful, restful and wonderful.

FILL THESE HEARTS WITH THE
PEOPLE OR THE THINGS YOU LOVE

HOW DO YOU FEEL TODAY?

Express yourself on this page.
Use pictures or words. They
don't have to make sense –
just think of the page as
a way to show how
you're feeling at
the moment.

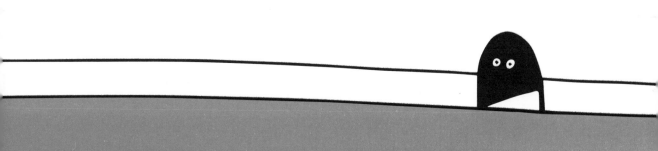

WRITE ABOUT YOUR DIFFERENT FEELINGS

When I feel **sad** I...

When I feel *ANGRY* I...

I am thankful for...

When I feel happy I...

COLOR THESE IN

Write down all the things that are important to you. You could write the most important things on the trunk of the tree and then work your way up.

CLOUD SHAPES

Lie down on a patch of grass outside, or gaze out the window on a cloudy day.

Look up at the clouds in the sky. What shapes can you see? Draw or describe them.

MORNING MANTRAS

Rather than thinking about your worries, it helps to focus each day on what you want to achieve instead. You can say these as morning mantras. (A mantra is like a watchword.) Then, at the end of the day, think about which of your mantras were successful, or how you could do better tomorrow.

Today, I will help a friend.

Today, I will learn something new.

THE PAGE FOR GROWN-UPS

This activity book is perfect for parents, teachers, learning mentors, caregivers, therapists and youth leaders who want to help children to understand and leave behind their worries.

Modern life for our children can be highly stressful, and they can feel like it's all about being popular and successful. We know that they experience many internal and external pressures, for example, comparing themselves with others around them and hearing news stories which they find themselves worrying about.

Children are very resilient, and in a loving and nurturing environment, will often work through problems and difficult times without needing additional help. This book offers the chance for your child to explore, express and explain their worries and open up the conversation with you. The activities foster resilience, increase inner calm, improve understanding of emotions and encourage positivity.

When children feel stuck with a problem, they may become lonely and isolated and struggle to make sense of what is happening because they don't have the language to explain their distress. You might notice a decline in self-esteem and confidence, along with complaints of stomachaches, headaches or feeling exhausted, as well as an avoiding of previously enjoyed activities.

If your child's anxiety or distress persists beyond three months or escalates rather than decreases, you can talk to their school, a doctor or a counselor.

NATIONAL ALLIANCE ON MENTAL ILLNESS (NAMI)

Educate, advocate, listen, lead.

The NAMI HelpLine can be reached Monday through Friday, 10 am-6 pm, ET.

NAMI is the nation's largest grassroots mental health organization dedicated to building better lives for the millions of Americans affected by mental illness.

www.nami.org

Tel: 1-800-950-NAMI (6264)
info@nami.org

GOODTHERAPY.ORG®

Helping people find therapists. Advocating for ethical therapy.

GoodTherapy.org offers a directory to help you in your search for a therapist. Using the directory, you can search by therapist location, specialization, gender, and age group treated. If you search by location, your results will include the therapists near you and will display their credentials, location, and the issues they treat.

Tel: 1-888-563-2112 ext. 1

www.goodtherapy.org

CHALLENGE THE STORM™

Sharing stories, resources and support for people facing emotional challenges.

Share your story and express yourself openly, and free from judgement.

www.challengethestorm.org

DR. SHARIE COOMBES